KT-525-000

LEAH MOHAMMED

LUMA
and the PET
the DRAGON

ILLUSTRATED BY LORETTA SCHAUER

WELBECK
FLAME

First published in 2022 by Welbeck Flame
An imprint of Welbeck Children's Limited,
part of Welbeck Publishing Group.
Based in London and Sydney.
www.welbeckpublishing.com

Text copyright © Leah Mohammed, 2022
Illustrations copyright © Loretta Schauer, 2022

Leah Mohammed and Loretta Schauer have asserted
their moral right to be identified as the Author
and Illustrator of this Work in accordance with the
Copyright Designs and Patents Act 1988.

ISBN: 978 1 80130 002 5

All rights reserved. No part of this publication may be
reproduced, stored in a retrieval system, or transmitted in
any form or by any means, electronically, mechanical,
photocopying, recording or otherwise, without the prior
permission of the copyright owners and the publishers.

Printed and bound by CPI Group (UK)

10 9 8 7 6 5 4 3 2 1

*For my beautiful daughter
and her constant love of dragons.*

The Birthday Surprise

Chapter One

Luma Dewan woke up on the morning of her seventh birthday.

'Today is the day!' she squealed, springing off her bed and doing two and a half jumps. (It would have been three jumps but one foot got accidentally left behind during the last jump.)

'TODAY IS THE DAY!'

And today *was* the day, but not just because it was Luma's birthday.

Today was special for a completely different reason. Today was the day Luma would be getting a puppy of her very own.

Except . . . not just any puppy, as it turned out.

Actually, not even a puppy at all.

But Luma didn't know that yet.

If she had known, it would have saved her quite a bit of deciding, because even though she had been waiting and waiting and *waiting* for today, she still was not entirely sure which puppy she was going to pick.

Luma grinned at the posters Mum had stuck to her wall.

Three fluffy puppies from the Forever Paws Rescue Centre stared back at her.

At first, Luma was sure she was going

to choose the brown one with dark blobs on its back. It had the kindest eyes and definitely looked like it would suit Luma's favourite name, Chloe.

But then Luma had caught sight of the grey puppy with curly fur. *It* had the cutest nose and also looked very much like a Chloe.

And then Luma completely changed her mind and decided the white puppy with the big floppy ears would be the one. (She looked even *more* like a Chloe.)

In fact, Luma had changed her mind every day since the rescue centre had sent the posters.

She had even tried her best to convince her mum that maybe they should bring all *three* home.

Luma reached up and stroked the nose of each puppy in turn.

There was only one thing Luma knew for certain.

By the time she went to sleep that night, Chloe would be with her and her heart would be full.

✦ ✹ ✦

Chapter Two

'Today is the day!'

Luma ran into her mum's bedroom and pounced.

Mum made a strange noise, a bit like the armbands Luma wore for swimming when she squashed out all the air.

Luma huffed.

She was going to have to do something she hadn't done in a long time, something she knew Mum really did not like.

'Mum! Mum! Mum!' Luma said, poking Mum's tummy.

One eye flicked open and glared.

Luma held her breath.

And then Mum's other eye popped open and . . .

'Happy birthday, seven-year-old Luma!' Mum smiled.

They went downstairs and right there on the little table in the living room was a tower of glittering silver presents.

'Yay!' Luma grinned. 'Can I open them?'

'You better had. Today *is* the day,' Mum said.

After that it was a whirl of torn silver paper.

One fluffy puppy bed!

A beautiful sparkling harness and lead!

Three puppy toys!

A matching food and water bowl!

And best of all, the pillow and blanket Mum had told Luma the puppy would *not* need and Luma had begged for.

'Thank you, thank you, thank you!' Luma said, hugging Mum tight. 'Can we go and get Chloe now?'

Mum looked at the clock and shook her head. 'It's still too early.'

'When will it *not* be too early?'

'Nine o'clock.'

'What time is it now?'

'Six thirty.'

'Oh.'

The hours took for ever.

Luma had already arranged Chloe's bed in her room, found the perfect spot for Chloe's pillow and blanket on the sofa in the living room, filled Chloe's bowls to bursting with puppy biscuits and water, and gone back to her room to rearrange Chloe's bed (it definitely looked much cosier next to hers) when finally, the little hand on the clock landed on the number nine.

'To Pet Rescue!' Luma and Mum cheered as they got in their car and then they were there, walking through the squeaky sliding doors.

'Slow down, Luma!' Mum called out, as Luma raced ahead.

'I can't!' she shouted back, and she really could not.

'Luma Dewan?' the lady behind the welcome desk asked as Luma skidded to a stop. 'What perfect timing! All the puppies are in the play room.'

Luma bounced on the spot.

A man wearing a bright blue Pet Rescue shirt led Luma and Mum all the way down a long blue corridor to a large blue door at the end.

He opened the door and . . .

'Puppies!' Luma zoomed inside.

Her eyes raced from one puppy to another. There was one with scruffy fur, a black puppy with a white mark on its paw, a brown spotty puppy and a completely yellow one, but . . .

'Where are *my* puppies?' Luma asked.

And then Mum, peering at one of the puppies rolling about on its back, said, 'I think, oh dear, that's a boy! They're all boys!'

'But Chloe is a girl,' Luma said.

'A girl?' the Pet Rescue man said. 'All the girl puppies went yesterday.'

'They can't have,' Luma said, feeling her bottom lip begin to tremble. 'I have a photo. I was supposed to pick!'

'I think there must have been a mix-up somewhere,' the Pet Rescue man said. 'Not to worry though, we'll have more puppies ready to leave in three weeks!'

Luma burst into tears. '*Today* . . . is . . . the . . . day!'

* ✷ *

Chapter Three

Luma and Mum returned home.

Luma couldn't bear to go into her room where the fluffy bed was waiting, or into the living room with the perfectly placed blanket and pillow, or even into the kitchen where she'd put the bowls of puppy biscuits and water.

'Why don't you go and see Nani?' Mum suggested. 'Yesterday she said she had a special present for you.'

Normally, Luma would have grinned at the thought of seeing her grandmother, *especially* today on her birthday, but right then there was nothing in the world that could have made her smile.

Luma pulled on her coat, stuck her feet in her garden wellies and opened the back door. Nani lived in the house next to theirs and there was a small gate in the fence between their gardens, for Luma to visit whenever she wanted.

Luma set off down the garden path, her eyes staring at her shuffling feet, her nose snuffling and the odd tear sliding down her cheek.

And then she felt the strangest feeling, a feeling like she wasn't alone, a feeling like she was being watched.

Luma stopped and looked around.

She couldn't see anything but she

heard a sound, a bit like a tweet or a tooting peep.

Luma stepped on to the wet, muddy grass and went to investigate. Maybe it was a bird fallen from its nest? Or even a baby fox, lost and needing someone to guide it home?

Luma peered around the plants and shrubs and bushes, all the way to the fence . . . there was nothing there.

'Oh.' Luma's shoulders slumped.

Of *course* there was nothing there.

She walked back to the path and had taken six steps this time when she heard another rustle and a small whispery whine, a whine so like a puppy that for a second Luma *did* smile.

She ran to where the noise had come from and there, right there! A flash of a long, grey tail!

'Chloe?' Luma said, because even though she knew it couldn't be, maybe, just maybe, Chloe had found her instead!

And then the plants, shrubs and bushes began moving as if something small was running through them.

'Chloe!'

Luma raced after it all the way to the tall, tall trees at the back of the garden.

Luma looked up and down and left and right, but she couldn't see a thing and worse, there were no more sounds, no bushes or plants moving and no feeling of something there, of being watched.

'No!' Luma cried. She ran to the gate and was through it in a shot, sprinting up Nani's garden until she was knocking on her back door.

* ✭ *

Chapter Four

'Happy birthday!' Nani cheered as she opened the door and then she saw the tears on Luma's cheeks. 'My Luma! What has happened?'

'We didn't . . . we didn't get Chloe!'

Nani dried Luma's eyes, led her to her armchair and pulled Luma on to her lap. 'Now, little one, tell me everything.'

Luma snuggled into her grandmother's arms and began to explain.

'And then the Pet Rescue man said we would have to wait three whole weeks for another puppy!'

'Oh my,' Nani said, but she didn't look quite as surprised or upset as Luma

thought she should be. 'Maybe a present would cheer you up?'

'I'm not sure anything could cheer me up ever again!'

'Is that so? Well, I suppose I don't *have* to give it you.'

'What? No!' Luma said. 'I would like a present.'

Nani chuckled and pointed to the dresser. 'It's in that drawer there.'

Luma jumped to her feet, opened the drawer and pulled out a small box wrapped in a sparkly purple ribbon. 'What is it?'

'Why don't you find out?'

Luma carefully untied the ribbon, opened the box and . . .

'Nani!' Luma said. 'But this is yours!'

For inside the box was Nani's gold charm bracelet, the one she never took off and had told Luma she'd had since *she* was a little girl.

'It is yours now,' Nani said. 'Here, let me put it on.'

Nani picked up the bracelet and fastened it around Luma's wrist.

'It is a bit big, but you will grow into it.' Nani smiled.

'Wow!' Luma turned her wrist back and forth, the five delicate charms glittering in the light. There was a beautiful, patterned heart charm, an odd-looking silver wing, sort of like a bat's but with a pointy claw on the top, an orb with a grey swirling stone inside, a silver locket with a small squiggle engraved on it and lastly,

Luma's favourite, a small black and gold dragon.

'Thank you, Nani.'

'You are very welcome,' Nani said and then she stood up. 'You should probably go home now.'

Luma frowned. 'But I just got here!'

'Or why don't you spend some time in my garden?' Nani carried on with a strange smile. 'It's a lovely day – you could make a mud pie, perhaps. Or look for newts in my pond?'

'OK,' Luma said slowly. 'But, Nani, why—'

'Off you go now. I'll be round later for your birthday tea!'

✶ ✹ ✶

Chapter Five

Nani had nearly pushed Luma out into the garden and then she had shut the door and, with a wave, disappeared.

Luma stared at the door. Nani was acting very oddly. First, giving Luma her precious bracelet and then sending her off when she knew Luma was still terribly upset *and* it was her birthday!

Luma huffed and set off across the grass. She didn't feel like playing in the garden at all, but she didn't want to go home either, not with all the puppy's things waiting for her.

Luma had just decided she would lie down on the trampoline and maybe

do some cloud spotting, when she felt
it again – that feeling like she wasn't
alone, that feeling like she was being
watched.

Luma spun around and there in
the bush right before her was a very
peculiar-looking nose, two large nostrils
twitching and sniffing and straining
towards her.

'Ah!' Luma cried.

And then a head emerged through the leaves, a grey scaly head with glittering silver eyes like a cat and two stubby horns either side of two very pointy ears.

'What are you?' Luma gasped.

The rest of the creature's body rushed out, triangle-shaped wings at its side and scaly grey claws and a tail, a very long, spiky tail, the spikes going all the way up its spine and the tip looking exactly like an arrow.

Luma's mouth dropped open. 'Dragon!'

'Want it,' the dragon said in a whispery voice. It pounced, tugging the charm bracelet over Luma's hand, and then it took off with a flutter of its wings!

Luma heard a crash from the other side of the fence. She opened the gate and raced through just in time to see the dragon's long, spiky tail vanish under the tall, tall trees.

'Give it back!' Luma shouted.

'Mine!' she heard the dragon say and then Luma had to stop and stand still because a *dragon* was in her garden! A real dragon *and* it talked!

Luma gulped and shook her head.

It may be a real talking dragon but it had stolen Nani's precious bracelet!

Chapter Six

Luma sprinted to the trees, got down on her knees and began to crawl through the leaves and branches.

'I know you're there – please give the bracelet back!'

'Mine! **Go away!**'

Luma found the dragon hunched by a wide tree trunk, one claw holding the bracelet and the other holding a strange, blue, spotted, leathery scrap.

'What is that?' Luma asked moving closer.

'Hiss!' the dragon hissed, scuffling backwards and tucking the leathery scrap and bracelet closer to its chest.

Luma stopped. She didn't want to scare the dragon away *or* get too close to those sharp, pointy claws. But how else could she get the bracelet back?

And then Luma had an idea.

'My name is Luma,' she said, shuffling an inch forward. 'What's your name?'

The dragon sniffed, its wings lifting and then it muttered, 'Timir.'

'Timir?' Luma said, and then she had to gulp and shake her head again because there was *a real talking dragon in her garden!*

'You are a dragon, aren't you? Where did you come from?' Luma asked in a rush. 'Dragons don't exist! Are there more somewhere? How old are you? And how can you talk?'

'Rah!' Timir growled. He spun in a circle and then curled up into a ball, his wings covering his head.

Luma bit her lip. She had at least a *thousand* more questions, but maybe it would be better to ask one at a time.

'I'm sorry, I didn't mean to scare you,' Luma said, starting up her shuffle towards him again. 'It's just I've never seen a dragon before.'

Timir's whole body shivered.
'Go away!'

'I can't go away,' Luma said and then she had the most peculiar feeling. Somehow, she knew, just *knew* she had been meant to find Timir. They already belonged together.

'You're here for me, aren't you?' Luma said.

Timir's wings slid slowly down from his face. 'I am here.'

But then he scowled and held up the leathery scrap. He gave it a long lick

and then held up the bracelet and gave that a large sniff. 'Mine.'

'Oh,' Luma said. She didn't really want to take the bracelet from him any more, but Nani had trusted her with it and she *had* to get it back.

Luma did one last shuffle and made a grab for the bracelet.

'No!' Timir wailed. 'I want it. Mine, mine, mine!'

✦ ✹ ✦

Chapter Seven

Timir tipped his head back and howled.

'Please don't cry! Here!' Luma said in a panic, dangling the bracelet in front of Timir (although her fingers were curled round the chain very tightly indeed). 'You can look at it!'

Timir scowled, his shoulders doing little whimpering judders and his nose twitching and snuffling. 'Need the smell!'

'What smell?' Luma sniffed the bracelet. There was a hint of Nani's perfume but nothing else, and then she caught sight of the little black and gold dragon charm.

How odd the bracelet had a dragon

charm when a real live dragon was sitting in front of her!

Luma thought about going back to Nani and telling her what she'd found, but then Luma remembered Nani insisting she leave and Luma didn't want to trouble her. She did, however, need some help.

Luma began to crawl backwards. 'I'm going to get Mum,' she told Timir. 'And maybe some food – you must be starving,' She thought about the little bowl filled to bursting with puppy biscuits. Luma felt a sharp twisting in her tummy then, but she soon smiled, for if she had got a puppy this morning, she would never have found Timir.

Clear of the branches and leaves,

Luma stood up and, to her surprise, found Timir right by her feet.

'Oh, you want to come too?' Luma asked.

Timir twisted the leathery scrap in his claws, his eyes locked on the bracelet.

Luma walked very slowly back down the path. She couldn't stop staring at Timir, especially now they were out in the bright daylight. It was, however, still quite hard to see him properly, as every few steps, Timir hopped and jumped, trying to get the bracelet back.

'We're here,' Luma said as they reached the back door. 'Mum is inside – she might be a bit shocked to see you, but don't be afraid.'

Timir stared up at her. 'Mum?' he whispered and then the strangest thing happened (*even* stranger than finding a dragon in your back garden) – Timir did a shake and began to transform before Luma's eyes!

Timir's wings tucked into his side, the spines on his back and the horns on his head disappearing as his body became covered in patchy grey fur.

His nose shortened, no longer a dragon's snout, but one looking very much like a dog's, and finally the arrow tip on his tail shrank away until it was just an ordinary fluffy dog's tail.

'You . . . you're a puppy!'

The back door swung open.

'Luma, you're back? What did Nani get you?' Mum asked, but then her eyes drifted down to Timir and she screamed.

Timir jumped with a loud, frightened, 'Rah!' and dashed through Mum's legs into the house!

'Timir!' Luma rushed inside after him.

Timir was racing round in panicked circles, jumping on the sofa and knocking off the cushions, banging into the

shelves and sending
books and ornaments
tumbling to the floor.

'Luma! Come here!'
Mum said, rushing to protect her.

'Timir!' Luma
shouted, trying to
run to Timir. 'Mum!
You're scaring him!'

Timir bashed into the small table on
the square rug and then he was gone,
down the hallway, knocking over their
shoe rack, and into Luma's bedroom.

'Why is there a *dog* in our house?'
Mum cried. 'Where did it come from?'

'A dog?' Luma said. She very much
wanted to tell Mum the truth, except
right that second she wasn't too sure
what the truth was.

'His name is Timir,' Luma said instead. 'I found him in the garden – actually, he found me. You gave him a real shock, Mum!'

'I gave *him* a shock!' Mum snorted and then her mouth dropped open. 'Did you say you found him in our garden?'

'Yes,' Luma said and then she sprinted off down the hallway to her room.

'Wait!' Mum called. 'Don't go in there! We need to call someone, animal control or the rescue centre – he could be dangerous!'

But Luma wasn't listening. She was worried about Timir. What if he'd hurt himself with all his crashing and bashing about?

* ✭ *

Chapter Eight

'Timir?' Luma looked around her bedroom. Everything was still neatly in its place. 'Where are you?'

'Luma!' Mum whispered, hovering in the doorway. 'Come out.'

And then Luma heard a snuffle from under her bed.

'Timir!' Luma turned upside down to peer underneath. She could just about make out a little grey splodge in the corner. 'You can come out. Everything's OK.'

'Everything is not OK!' Mum said.

'Please, Mum, he's very scared.' Luma stood up and rummaged about in her

250 pcs
UNICOF

toy chest, pulling out her unicorn torch.
'Here, have a look.'

Mum let out a very large huff, but she
came in, kneeling beside Luma to see.

Timir was huddled in the corner,
his little body shaking and quivering.

'What an odd-looking dog!' Mum said. 'Look at its patchy fur and strange head. And what is it holding in its paw?'

'I'm not sure,' Luma said. 'But he's not odd, he's amazing and way better than the puppies from the rescue centre.'

'What do you mean?' Mum's eyes narrowed.

'Because he's mine now,' Luma said.

'But . . .' Mum's mouth opened and shut and opened again. 'I thought you were desperate for a girl?'

'I changed my mind,' Luma said. 'Please, Mum, please! I was supposed to find him, I just know it, and after this morning . . .' Luma's last words turned into a hiccup.

Mum looked under the bed again.

'I can't believe I'm saying this,' Mum

said. 'But maybe you *were* supposed to find him? I mean, what are the chances?'

'Yay!' Luma cheered. 'Did you hear that, Timir, you can stay!'

'Wait! I didn't say you could keep him,' Mum said. 'We will have to make sure he doesn't belong to anyone else first.'

'He doesn't, I know it. He's mine,' Luma said.

★ ★ ★

Chapter Nine

'Timir?' Luma called. 'You really can come out now.'

'Yes, I would like a better look at him,' Mum said. 'What an unusual name! However did you think of that?'

'Err...' Luma didn't know *what* to say.

'Maybe we should try tempting him out with food,' Mum said.

'Oh yes!' Luma hopped up, sprinted to the kitchen and was back again in a flash, a trail of puppy biscuits left behind.

'Right, let's put it here and see if he

comes out,' Mum said, placing the bowl in front of the bed.

Timir's nose emerged, twitching and sniffing, and then a rather large pointy tongue poked out and sucked up two biscuits.

There was a crunch and . . . one biscuit came back, shooting across Luma's bedroom and pinging off the rocket she had made from old cardboard boxes.

'Yuck! I do not like that!' Timir said.

Luma looked at Mum to see if she'd understood what Timir had said, but Mum was staring at where Timir's nose had appeared, slowly shaking her head.

'What a pointy tongue he has,' Mum said. 'And what strange noises he makes!'

Luma was desperate to tell Mum that Timir was not actually a puppy but a dragon disguised as a puppy, but if Mum couldn't see Timir as he really was or hear Timir talk, how would Luma be able to convince her?

'What else could we try?' Mum asked.

Luma wasn't sure, but then . . . of course! She needed to *talk* to Timir, tell him everything was OK and listen to his worries, just like Mum did with her whenever she was afraid.

There was only one problem: Luma didn't think she could do any of that in front of Mum.

'Aren't Nani and Auntie and my cousins coming soon?' Luma asked.

'Oh yes,' Mum said, looking a bit panicked. 'I haven't even started on your birthday tea yet!'

Mum stood up and was about to leave when she turned back. 'I think you should come too, Luma. We still don't know anything about the puppy – he might not be safe.'

'He is safe, I know he is,' Luma said. 'And he needs me to calm him down and keep an eye on him in case he does come out.'

'Fine,' Mum sighed. 'But if anything happens, anything at all, come and get me at once. And we're leaving your bedroom door *wide* open!'

✦ ✹ ✦

Chapter Ten

As soon as Mum left, Luma lay down on the carpet.

'Mum has gone, we can talk now.'

But Timir did not reply.

Luma picked up her torch and shone it under the bed and there were Timir's wings again, his long dragon snout, his tail with an arrow at the end, and his scales shimmering under the light.

'Are you a dragon *and* a dog? Or are you just a dragon pretending to be a dog? Why are you hiding from Mum? And why can't she hear you talk?'

Timir glared back at her. 'Go away,'

he said, and then he bent his head and nuzzled his leathery scrap.

'But—'

'Go away!' Timir roared.

Luma sat up. Why was Timir being mean? He'd talked to her in the garden and followed her into the house and now he was telling her to go away. And what *was* that strange scrap Timir was holding?

And then Luma spotted one of the new puppy toys she'd unwrapped this morning.

'Oooh!' Luma grabbed the plush monkey with knotted ropes for arms and legs and hopped on to her bed, dangling it over the side.

'Timir? What's this?'

Luma heard the sound of shuffling underneath her.

It was working!

Luma waved the toy faster and faster and . . . **Whoosh!**

The toy disappeared under the bed with Timir.

There was a loud ripping sound followed by ferocious biting and growling.

'I get it!'

Clouds of fluff and shredded pieces flew out on to the carpet.

'Oh,' Luma sighed. That hadn't worked at all. What was she going to do now?

And then the doorbell rang.

★ ✷ ★

Chapter Eleven

'They're here!' Mum called. 'Early for once, as well!'

Luma sprang to her feet, just in time to see Mum rushing past her room towards the front door.

'Puppy! Puppy!' Reyansh, Luma's younger cousin, shouted as he raced down the hallway towards her.

'Where's the puppy, Luma?' Arjun, Luma's older cousin, asked, sprinting in front of Reyansh.

'We came early,' Luma heard Auntie tell Mum. 'The boys are so excited . . . **Luma! Happy birthday!**'

Auntie swept Luma up into a big squishy hug.

'The puppy, Luma?' Arjun asked.

And then Nani appeared.

'Hello again.' Nani smiled. 'How was your play in the garden, Luma? Did you find anything interesting?'

'The puppy!' Arjun and Reyansh shouted together. 'Where is the puppy?'

'Oh . . . he's in my room,' Luma said, and then seeing the eager looks on Arjun and Reyansh's faces, she quickly shut her bedroom door.

'*He*?' Auntie said. 'I thought you wanted a girl?'

'A boy puppy, brilliant.' Arjun grinned, reaching for the door handle.

'No!' Luma said, batting his hand away. 'We didn't get him from the rescue centre,' Luma explained. 'I found him in the garden and he's very scared.'

'In the garden?' Auntie said. 'How odd!'

'I know!' Mum said.

'Please let us see him, Luma, please!' Reyansh wailed.

'They might help to encourage Timir out of hiding,' Mum said.

'I doubt it,' Luma said and then she sighed and opened the door.

'He's under the bed,' Luma said.

'What's all this mess?' Auntie asked, eyeing the torn-up bits of monkey toy.

'I thought he might like a play,' Luma said. 'But he ripped it up instead.'

'I can't see him,' Reyansh said, kneeling down in front of Luma's bed.

'Move over!' Arjun shoved Reyansh aside. 'There's nothing there.'

'There is,' Luma said. 'There's a . . .
err, puppy.'

And then Reyansh spotted Luma's
torch and turned it on.

There was a loud hiss.

'I see him!'

'Go away!' Timir roared.

Luma leapt on Reyansh and took the

torch. 'I knew you'd scare him!'

'What was that noise?' Auntie asked. 'It sounded like a bird squawking or a cat screeching!'

'That's what I thought,' Mum said.

'I need to have a look,' Auntie said, kneeling beside the boys, and then she gasped. 'What an odd-looking dog!'

'What about this?' Arjun asked, pulling out a light-up yo-yo from his pocket. 'I bet the puppy will come out for this.'

'I wouldn't,' Luma warned.

Arjun rolled the yo-yo under the bed.

'Attack!' Timir cried.

'Ow!' Arjun shouted as the string disappeared. 'My yo-yo!'

'I told you so,' Luma said, crossing her arms.

'A net!' Arjun scowled. 'We could trap

him and drag him out.'

'Never!' Luma shouted.

'I can fit underneath,' Reyansh said, dropping to his tummy and wiggling forward.

'No!' Mum grabbed Reyansh's feet and tugged him backwards.

'Well,' said a voice behind them. 'He's never going to come out with you all crowded around.'

Everyone turned to look at Nani.

* ✱ *

Chapter Twelve

Luma's grandmother was sitting calmly in Luma's purple flowery chair.

Luma frowned.

Why had Nani been so keen for her to play in the garden earlier?

It was almost as if Nani knew she would find Timir.

'Boys, why don't you go outside and look for newts in my pond? There were some hatching earlier,' Nani said, standing up. 'And my girls, how about a cup of tea?'

'Yes, tea would be lovely,' Mum said. 'It has been quite a morning!'

'Listen to your nani,' Auntie said, as the boys began to protest.

'Now, my Luma,' Nani said once the bedroom door finally closed. (Auntie had had to carry Reyansh away.) 'Where is the bracelet?'

Luma slipped it off her wrist and passed it to Nani, once again catching sight of the gold and black dragon charm. 'Nani! What is going on?'

Nani sat on Luma's bed and patted the space beside her.

'I have been waiting for this day for a very, *very* long time.'

'You have?' Luma asked.

'First, what is his name?'

'Timir!' Timir peeped from under the bed.

'Timir! What a fine name,' Nani said.

'It is, isn't it?' Luma said and then she gasped. 'Wait! Nani, you can hear him talk too. Does that mean . . . do you know, he's not a puppy at all, he's a—'

'Dragon.' Nani grinned.

'But how? Where did he come from? Dragons don't exist, and why can he change into a puppy and why can't anyone else hear him speak and how did you know I was going to find him, because you *did* know, didn't you?'

'So many questions and so much to tell you,' Nani said. 'But first, the charm bracelet . . . you see, Luma, this is no ordinary bracelet.'

'It's not?' Luma asked.

'No, it is magic . . . well, a little bit of magic and little bit of something else, like this charm here,' Nani said, pointing to the orb with the grey swirling stone. 'It has something very special inside,

something no dragon can resist.'

'So that's why he stole it *and* kept sniffing it!' Luma said. 'But it's been on my wrist since we came in the house and Timir is still hiding!'

'Steal it, did he?' Nani laughed. 'It must be working then . . . maybe if we hold it closer to him?'

Nani passed the bracelet back to Luma.

Luma got off the bed and knelt near to where Timir was hiding.

'Here, Timir,' she said, waving the bracelet back and forth.

Luma heard a very large snort and the next moment, Timir was almost sitting in her lap, trying to bite the bracelet out of her hand.

'Mine!' Timir cried.

'Oh! What a beauty he is!' Nani said.

Timir stopped and turned around, his eyes narrowing as he stared at Nani. He gripped his leathery scrap even tighter and, with a shake of his head, returned back under the bed.

'Hmm,' Nani said. 'What was that in his claws? I think ... ah, it must be a part of his *chilka*, his eggshell.'

'So that's what it is!' Luma said. 'He's been holding on to it ever since I found him.'

'Maybe that is why he won't come out,' Nani said. 'He must be protecting it.'

'But I don't want to take it,' Luma said.

'Of course,' Nani said. 'But Timir might not know that.'

'Oh,' Luma said. She lay down and

wriggled forward so she could see Timir. 'It's OK, Timir, I won't take your eggshell. You can leave it under the bed and it will be safe.'

'Not safe,' Timir muttered. 'Go away.'

Luma looked up at Nani. 'What can we do?'

Nani shook her head. 'I'm not sure, little one.'

Luma frowned.

She was thinking very hard.

'What if . . .'

Luma stood up and walked to her bookshelf. There in the middle was the music box that Nana, her grandfather, had given her. Luma picked the music box up and closed her eyes and, just like every time she held it, she remembered Nana. His warm hand on her head, his tight hugs and deep laugh and his voice when he told her he loved her.

'I have an idea,' Luma told Nani.

* ✷ *

Chapter Thirteen

Luma sat back down and placed the music box in front of her.

'Timir?' Luma said. 'My nana, my granddad, is gone too. He gave me this before he . . . before he died. It is very precious to me. My most precious thing ever, just like your eggshell. Maybe you could put it inside here to keep it safe. Both our precious things together.'

Luma opened the music box, the little ballerina twirling to life as soft, twinkling music filled Luma's bedroom.

Timir wriggled out from under the bed.

He sat in front of the music box and lifted one claw.

'Remember, Timir,' Luma said. 'It is very, *very* precious.'

Timir looked at Luma. 'Your precious?'

'Yes, Timir.'

Timir turned back to the box and then very carefully poked the ballerina, cooing as it sprang back and carried on its graceful loops.

'It's OK, I promise your eggshell will be safe in here.'

Timir stared at his leathery scrap. He lifted it up and gave it a lick.

'Mine,' he said.

'I know.'

'Keep it safe?'

'I promise.'

And then Timir stretched his claw forward, gently dropping his leathery scrap next to the ballerina.

Luma closed the lid. 'I will put it back, Timir,' she said, picking up the box. 'And you will always know where it is.'

Timir watched Luma place the music box on the shelf and then spun around in a circle and dived into Luma's pile of teddies.

'Fluffies!' he said, rolling about on his back and biting teddy arms and legs.

'Oh, no!' Luma said, remembering what had happened to the monkey toy. 'You can't bite those.'

Timir jumped up and ran towards Luma's bookshelf, his claws digging into

Luma's encyclopaedia and pulling it on to the floor.

'I get it!' Timir cried, leaping on top of the book and scrabbling at the cover.

'Not that either,' Luma said, trying to wrestle it from him.

Timir's head shot up as he looked

about Luma's room. His eyes had just locked on Luma's marble tower, when Nani stepped in.

'Calm now, Timir,' Nani said, picking him up.

'Rah!' Timir said, but then he let out a sleepy yawn. 'Luma,' he said, reaching towards her.

Nani passed Timir to Luma.

She sat down on the bed, cuddling him in her arms.

'What a lovely idea that was with the music box,' Nani said, sitting next to them. 'And now Timir knows his eggshell is safe, he can be with you.'

Luma grinned. 'Did Nana know about dragons too?'

'No, he did not,' Nani said.

'But how do you know about them, Nani?' Luma said. 'And why is Timir here? Where did he come from?'

'Well, Luma,' Nani said. 'That is a mystery!'

✦ ✸ ✦

Chapter Fourteen

'Nobody knows where the dragons come from or why,' Nani explained. 'Only that for as long as anyone can remember in our family, every fifty years or so, a baby dragon arrives for us to care for.'

'Wow!' Luma grinned, but then her smile faded. 'Why can't Timir be a dragon in front of Mum, or Auntie and my cousins, then?'

'Ah,' Nani said. 'It is only the ones who have *found* a dragon who can see them that way. When anyone else is about, as you know, they change.'

'But I don't want to lie, especially to Mum,' Luma said.

'I know, but Timir is a puppy to her and to everyone else. That *is* the truth and he must live and be trained exactly as a young dog would.'

'And I will definitely need Mum's help for that,' Luma said, trying to grab her jumper sleeve from Timir's nibbling mouth. 'I think he is quite cheeky, actually.'

'Yes, indeed,' Nani chuckled. 'There is a lot of other stuff he must learn too. I will help you with that.'

'There is?'

'Why yes, all manner of dragon things!'

Timir yawned (finally letting go of Luma's sleeve), his eyes blinking and blinking until they shut.

'And what about the bracelet, Nani?' Luma asked, softly stroking Timir's fluffy back. 'Where did it come from and what do the other charms do?'

'Well, the bracelet was found with the very first dragon and it has been passed down ever since,' Nani said. 'And as for what the charms do . . . just know they will help you when you need them the most.'

Then there were footsteps outside Luma's room.

Timir sat up, suddenly wide awake. He did a big shake and was no longer a dragon but the puppy from before.

'You got him out of hiding then,' Mum said, coming in and sitting down next to Luma. 'He is a scruffy thing, isn't he, Ammi?'

'Yes, he could do with a bath,' Nani chuckled.

'Bath?' Timir said, tilting his head.

'Aw, he does seem very sweet, though,' Mum said, reaching forward to stroke Timir's ears.

'Yes, he is, and lovely and wonderful and absolutely amazing!' Luma said.

Mum laughed. 'Now, is anyone hungry because I think we are just about ready for your birthday tea.'

'I'm hungry!' Timir said.

* ✳ *

Chapter Fifteen

Luma carried Timir into the kitchen, grinning as she caught sight of the table crammed with all her favourite food. Mini pizzas and fish fingers, a stack of warm chapattis and a bowl of fragrant dal, a mound of popcorn and a plate full of oozing cheese toasties, but best of all, a gigantic, glistening chocolate cake in the middle, seven candles and a sparkler on top.

'Wow! Thank you, Mum!'

'Yummy!' Timir cried, twisting in Luma's arms to reach for the food.

'Not for you,' Nani said, tickling Timir under his chin.

'Puppy!' Reyansh cried, crashing into

the kitchen, Arjun just behind. 'Can I touch him, please, please, please!'

'I want to hold him!' Arjun said, pushing Reyansh out of the way to get closer to Timir.

'Boys! You are frightening him,' Nani said. 'Now, Luma, pass Timir to me and let's make a start on your birthday tea.'

Luma and her family sat down and soon it was a blur of reaching arms and happy munching mouths until the bowls and plates were all but scraped clean.

'He really is odd-looking, isn't he?' Auntie said, frowning at Timir.

'I wonder where he came from?' Arjun asked.

'I wish I could find a puppy in our garden,' Reyansh whined, trying to reach across Luma to touch Timir in Nani's lap.

Timir wasn't paying the slightest attention. His eyes were locked on the last mini pizza, his tongue poking out, further and further towards the plate.

Luma giggled. She took the mini pizza, bit it in half and very sneakily passed it over to Timir.

'Luma!' Nani tutted.

'We saw that,' Mum said.

Timir sat back in Nani's arms and licked his lips. 'Yum!'

'Is it time for cake?' Reyansh asked.

'And tea,' Nani said. 'I never did get mine earlier.'

Luma shut her eyes tight as the candles were lit and the cake placed before her.

'Come on,' Luma heard Arjun say. 'The candles will melt into the chocolate.'

'I'm thinking of a wish,' Luma said, because what could she possibly wish for now she had a dragon?

But then she smiled.

'Of course,' she whispered.

I wish to be together with Timir, always and for ever.

Luma opened her eyes, took a deep breath and blew.

All the candles but one went out.

'I'll do it.' Timir sat up on Nani's lap.

He took a deep breath and blew and then . . . leapt on to the table and chomped down on the cake, gobbling up two candles as well.

'Timir!'

✦ ✦ ✦

Chapter Sixteen

Later in the evening, after Luma's cake had been eaten (Mum had rescued it from Timir), and tea had been drunk (mostly by Nani), and Luma, Timir and Mum had waved goodbye to Nani, Auntie and the boys (Reyansh did *not* want to go), and a bath had been had (Timir stole two rubber ducks!), Mum tucked Luma into bed.

'Well, what a day!' Mum said. 'Are you happy, Luma?'

'I am very happy, Mum,' Luma said, grinning down at Timir on his bed.

'Well, good night, my seven-year-old Luma.' Mum bent down to kiss Luma's forehead. 'And good night, Timir.'

'Good night, Mum.'

Luma waited until her bedroom door closed and then . . .

'You can come up now.'

Timir jumped on to the bed and snuggled down next to Luma under the covers.

'Sleepy,' Timir purred and a second later he was fast asleep, his little mouth hanging open as he snuffled and snored.

It took Luma a little bit longer to fall asleep herself.

At first, she couldn't stop staring at Timir.

What an adventure it had been already!

Luma looked at her music box and smiled. She was glad both their precious things were together and now Timir was her best friend.

Timir let out a particularly large snort.

Luma felt her eyes grow heavy.

She cuddled Timir and smiled.

Whatever happened, she had been right.

Today *was* the day.

Timir was with her and her heart was so very full.

★ ✹ ★

The Puppy-Training Class

Chapter One

Luma woke up to the feeling of something heavy resting on her chest.

She did a few sleepy blinks and found two glittering silver eyes staring right at her.

'Luma awake!'

'No, Timir,' she mumbled. 'It's too early. I can feel it.'

A wet nose nudged her cheek.

Luma groaned and rolled over.

Timir tumbled off Luma's tummy. 'Luma, wake up now,' he said, wriggling under her arms and trying to lick her face.

Luma turned on to her front. She heard Timir whine and jump off the bed and then . . . silence.

She let out a happy sigh and was just starting to fall back to sleep when there was a loud ripping noise.

Luma sat up at once.

Timir was lying on her rug, his mouth wide open and about to chomp down on her favourite teddy.

Luma leapt out of bed.

Her teddy collection had shrunk quite a bit since she found Timir in her garden a week ago and she didn't want to lose another one, especially her favourite zebra teddy.

'Luma is awake!' Timir cheered and then he started on his morning zoomies.

'Timir, please, we've talked about this: my teddies are not toys,' Luma said, trying to keep track of Timir as he jumped and raced about her room.

And then she caught sight of the clock on her bedside table.

Luma wasn't sure what it said exactly, but she did know that the small hand was only just past the number five.

'I knew it was too early!' Luma said. 'We're not supposed to be awake until six. Remember what Mum said?'

Timir did not listen. He let out a little roar, doing one last lap of her room before coming to a sharp stop. 'Tummy hungry.'

Luma huffed. She knew there would be no going back to sleep now.

She slipped out of her room, down the hall, and into the kitchen, Timir following close behind.

Using the stool, she reached into the high cupboard to grab the box of her favourite cereal.

'Mine!' Timir said, bouncing up and down.

'What about your puppy food?'

'Yucky,' Timir said.

'But . . .' Luma shook her head. They'd had this same conversation again and again and it always ended in Timir eating *her* food.

Luma got two bowls and one spoon.

'Come on then, let's watch the telly.'

Chapter Two

'Luma? Timir?'

Luma woke for the second time that morning, her mum's face smiling above her.

She had a moment of worry that Timir had fallen asleep as a dragon. But a quick glance down showed him curled up at her side as a puppy, grey and fluffy with two very large, pointy ears.

'Did Timir wake you up again?' Mum asked.

'Yes.' Luma nodded, stroking Timir's soft head as he let out a yowling yawn.

'Maybe he should sleep in the living room,' Mum said.

'Oh no!' Luma said. 'He will get lonely and I will get lonely too.'

Mum frowned. 'Well, we will need to work on that *and* Timir eating his own breakfast,' she said, eyeing up the milky remains in the two bowls.

Timir scooted forward on the sofa and was getting ready to slurp up the leftovers when Mum took the bowls away.

'But I am hungry!' Timir said. 'Luma? When is more food?'

Luma had to wait until Mum had wandered off to the kitchen to answer Timir. Just like how Luma and her nani were the only ones Timir could be a dragon around, they were also the only ones able to hear him speak.

'We have already had our breakfast,' she told him. 'You will have to wait.'

Timir grumbled. 'But my tummy is so empty.'

'What should we do today?' she asked, hoping to take Timir's mind off his stomach.

Timir sat up straight, his eyes pinned to the back door. Luma leant around him to see what he had seen and there, in the middle of the garden, was a . . .

squirrel! Timir roared.

Timir flew off the sofa, his front paws crashing into the door with a bang. 'Let me out! Squirrel! I get it!'

'What's going on?' Mum said, rushing into the living room.

'A squirrel,' Luma said, walking over to Timir and trying to pick him up. Timir dodged Luma's hands, his puppy woofs turning into wails as the squirrel ran away.

'Ah,' Mum said, bending down and scooping Timir up. 'You can't chase squirrels,' she told him, gently stroking his tummy.

'I want the squirrel,' Timir said, but it came out more as a purr, as he went floppy in Mum's arms.

Timir could not resist a tummy tickle.

'Mum?' Luma asked. 'What should we do today?'

'I have to go into work,' Mum said, putting Timir down. 'Remember, I told you yesterday?'

Luma frowned. She did not remember.

'You are going to Nani's for the day.'

'Yay!' Luma grinned.

'Nani!' Timir said, spinning in a circle.

Mum laughed. 'Why don't you pack a bag with things you would like to take?'

Luma skipped to her bedroom, Timir weaving through her legs and very nearly tripping her up.

Inside their room, Luma grabbed her backpack. 'What should we bring, Timir?'

Timir gave a shake, changing into his dragon form, and then trotted off towards her big tub of building blocks.

'No,' Luma said. 'It's far too heavy

and anyway, you always destroy anything I make.'

'I do not,' Timir said.

Luma heard the phone ring in the distance and her mum's footsteps as she walked to answer it.

'I wonder who that is?' Luma asked.

Timir picked up the plastic sword Luma was given when she'd been a knight for dress-up day at school.

'No,' Luma said. 'It won't fit in the bag and sword-fighting makes you far too growly.'

Timir walked over to a grey teddy and was about to pick it up when he shook and changed back into a puppy.

⋆ ✷ ⋆

Chapter Three

Luma's bedroom door opened.

'That was your auntie,' Mum said. 'Your cousins will be with Nani for a couple of hours this morning too.'

'Urgh,' Luma said as Mum closed the door.

'Cousins?' Timir asked.

'Remember the two boys?' Luma said. 'The day we found each other, you were hiding under the bed and they tried to get you out, remember, with the—'

'Yo-yo,' Timir said, his eyes growing larger. He shot under the bed and was out a second later, the remains of Arjun's yo-yo in his mouth.

The yo-yo had become one of Timir's favourite toys, but it was now in tatters, the string broken off and lost, the plastic case chewed all along the sides.

'Another yo-yo?' Timir asked.

'Maybe,' Luma said. 'Right, I have decided. We will take our new colouring book and fancy pens, one jigsaw puzzle, my recorder – remember, I have to practise, but I will take the drum too so you can play along with me and . . . this teddy, I suppose, but you are not allowed to bite her at all, Timir!'

Luma zipped up her backpack and hefted it over to her door.

'All ready, then?' Mum asked.

'Yes.' Luma smiled, handing Mum her backpack and picking up Timir.

'Oof! What have you got in there?' Mum laughed. 'And what about Timir's harness and lead?'

So far Timir hadn't been convinced by his harness and lead at all.

'Um, they're in my bag . . . I thought I would carry him or I could go through the garden?' Luma asked.

Luma always thought she was very lucky to live right next door to her grandmother, especially as it meant she had two gardens to play in and could visit Nani whenever she liked.

'We have to go out the front – I'm wearing my work shoes,' Mum said. 'You carry him, but make sure you hold on tight.'

✶ ✦ ✶

Chapter Four

Mum knocked on Nani's front door.

'Oh dear,' Mum said to Luma as they heard shouts coming from inside the house. 'It seems your cousins are already here.'

Luma groaned. She wished her cousins were not here at all, and her arms were starting to ache from holding Timir. 'Should we knock again?'

The door swung open.

Nani stood before them, Reyansh on one side and Arjun on the other.

'Luma and Timir!' Nani grinned. 'Come on in – we were just settling a little disagreement.'

'I should be allowed to play with Timir

first because I am the oldest,' Arjun said.

'No, I should be first because I am the youngest!' Reyansh shouted.

'Maybe Luma should decide as Timir is her . . . dog,' Nani said, with a little wink to Luma.

Luma smiled at Nani, though she couldn't hold it for long. She didn't want either of her cousins to play with Timir, but Timir wriggled in her arms.

'Yo-yo?' he asked, straining towards Arjun.

'I'll leave you all to it,' Mum said, giving Luma a big hug. 'Be good for Nani . . . and that means you too, Arjun and Reyansh!'

Luma waved as Mum left and then they were inside Nani's house.

'Now, why don't you all go out in the garden? I have a cup of tea waiting for me

and a crossword to finish,'
Nani said, leading the way
to her back door.

'But I want to play with
Timir!' Reyansh cried.

'And so you will,' Nani
said. 'In the garden.'

Luma did not feel like playing at all.
She was still feeling sleepy from
Timir waking her up so early, even with
the little nap they'd had together after
breakfast.

Luma stared hopefully at the sofa.
Maybe the boys could go outside and she
and Timir could cuddle up under Nani's
woven blanket and watch cartoons?

But, as soon as the boys ran outside,
Timir leapt out of her arms and raced
after them.

Luma gave the sofa a longing look and followed Timir and her cousins outside.

'Look at Timir!' Arjun said, walking backwards.

Timir was jumping up and down at Arjun's side, doing fierce snorting sniffs.

'What's he doing?' Reyansh asked. 'Do it to me, Timir!'

'Yo-yo!' Timir said, rather muffled as he managed to fit his entire nose inside Arjun's pocket.

'It tickles!' Arjun giggled, trying to push Timir away.

'Do you have another yo-yo?' Luma asked Arjun.

'No,' Arjun said. 'Why?'

Timir flumped to the ground, his little mouth wobbling.

Luma knew what was coming next and

she also knew that she could not let Arjun and Reyansh see Timir cry. It was not exactly dog-like and Nani had told Luma more than once how important it was for Timir to act like the puppy he appeared to be around others.

Luckily Arjun turned away, right as Timir opened his mouth to let the first wailing cry out.

'Let's go on the trampoline, my turn first,' Arjun said, running to the gate that connected Luma's and Nani's gardens.

'Timir? Do you want to bounce?' Luma asked.

Timir let out the breath he'd been sucking in and wagged his tail. 'Bounce, bounce!' he said, setting off after Arjun.

Luma quickly followed them.

As soon as Arjun opened the zip

on the large mesh surrounding the trampoline, Timir whizzed past him.

By the time Arjun had climbed inside, Timir was happily bouncing, higher and higher, little squeaks coming out with each bounce.

Luma giggled. Timir loved the trampoline.

But Arjun stood with his hands on his hips, a big scowl on his face. 'Dogs don't bounce on trampolines.'

'Yes, they do,' Luma said. 'Lots of dogs bounce on trampolines.'

'They do not,' Arjun said. 'My friend Thomas has two dogs and I've been to his house six times and not once have I seen his dogs on his trampoline . . .'

Chapter Five

Luma looked at Timir and gulped.

Maybe Arjun was right and dogs didn't bounce on trampolines?

'Make him stop,' Arjun said. 'It's my turn, anyway.'

Luma ran to Timir.

'Timir,' she whispered. 'Don't jump on the trampoline.'

Timir did not listen.

He carried on bouncing until he caught sight of Reyansh carrying a bucket full of sloppy mud into Nani's garden, and burst out of the trampoline to Reyansh's side.

Luma rushed after them.

As soon as Reyansh put the bucket

down, Timir sat up on his hind legs and pushed his two front paws deep into the squelchy mud.

'What's he doing?' Arjun asked, his head appearing over the fence.

'Just playing,' Luma said.

But then Reyansh wandered off and came back with one of Nani's old baking trays.

'Let's make a mud pie,' Reyansh said.

Timir squealed, digging out a pawful of mud and flinging it into the tray.

Luma looked towards where Arjun was bouncing up and down. She wasn't sure dogs made mud pies, but Arjun was busy trying to grab leaves off a nearby tree.

'What a good boy.' Reyansh grinned after they'd filled the tray up and were patting down the top to make it firm and smooth. 'This is an excellent pie! Let's tip it out and make another one!'

'Dogs don't make mud pies,' Luma heard Arjun call.

She twisted around, her heart sinking.

'Timir,' Luma whispered. 'You had better stop.'

But Timir did not hear her.

And then a yellow tennis ball flew past them.

Timir raised his head, watching as the ball landed by one of Nani's flower beds.

He did not run after it.

'All dogs love balls,' Arjun said, coming through the gate towards them. 'Why isn't Timir chasing it?'

'Um. . .' Luma didn't know what to say, so *she* ran after the ball. She was starting to feel very worried. It seemed Timir was not acting like a dog at all!

Chapter Six

Luma grabbed the ball off the ground and threw it. 'Get the ball, Timir!'

Timir didn't even notice – he was far too busy helping Reyansh tip out their second mud pie.

Luma looked at Arjun.

Arjun was staring at Timir.

'My turn on the trampoline,' Reyansh called, wiping his sticky, muddy hands down his shorts.

Timir tried to do the same, wiping his sticky, muddy paws down Luma's jeans.

And then Timir froze, his eyes locked on something near the fence.

'Oh no,' Luma said.

'Squirrel!' Timir roared and he was gone.

Luma shook her head, although at least Arjun couldn't say anything about Timir chasing a squirrel. She was almost absolutely sure *all* dogs did that.

She was just about to start after Timir when a soft glow caught her eye.

Luma glanced around but she couldn't see where the light was coming from. She walked through the gate into her own garden, towards the tall, tall trees and Timir's cries of 'Squirrel! I want you!'

The light was shining brighter.

Luma spun in a circle.

Where *was* it coming from?

And then the light changed from a glow to a bright, blinding flash.

Timir shot out from the trees, shaking dirt and leaves off his back.

'Squirrel gone,' he grumbled.

'That's probably for the best,' Luma said, still trying to find the light but it seemed to have disappeared.

'Luma! Boys!' Luma heard Nani call. 'Time for a snack!'

'Snack!' Timir licked his lips.

'Timir, wait! We need to talk,' Luma said.

But Timir did not hear. He raced back through the gate into Nani's garden.

Luma sighed and starting walking.

By the time Luma made it inside, Arjun, Reyansh and Timir were sitting on the sofa. The boys had glasses of Nani's homemade lemonade in one hand and a chocolate-chip biscuit in the other.

'Mine?' Timir asked, pushing on to Reyansh's lap and biting at the air around his biscuit.

Luma froze. Dogs did not eat chocolate-chip biscuits.

'Let's put the telly on,' Luma said.

Timir loved cartoons and it would distract him from the food.

Luma reached for the remote and scooped Timir up to sit on her lap.

'Look, Timir,' Luma said.

Timir was wriggling against her, his eyes still firmly on Reyansh's biscuit.

But then the music from his favourite programme began to play.

'Ooh!' Timir cooed, turning his head towards the TV.

Soon Timir was mesmerised, letting out woofs and squeaks at all the funny bits.

Luma reached for her biscuit and was about to take her first bite, when Arjun spoke.

'Dogs don't watch TV.'

'Of course they do,' Luma said. That was a completely normal thing for a dog to do, wasn't it?

'They don't,' Arjun said. 'My friend's dogs don't watch TV.'

'Oh,' Luma said. She put her biscuit back on the plate. She did not feel hungry at all now.

What was she supposed to do?

* ✹ *

Chapter Seven

It wasn't much longer before Auntie arrived and soon Luma was happily waving goodbye to Arjun and his suspicious looks.

'Nani,' Luma said as soon as Nani shut the front door. 'Timir is not acting like a dog today!'

'Oh dear,' Nani said. 'Is that right, Timir?'

Timir snorted and changed into his dragon self.

'Timir is dragon!' he said, puffing out his chest.

'And that's the other thing,' Luma said. 'Timir won't listen to me when I tell him not to do something!'

'I do,' Timir said.

'You do not,' Luma said. 'Like this morning, I said it was too early to get up and to not rip up my teddies. And I told you to stop bouncing on the trampoline and to stop making mud pies and I told you to chase the ball because all dogs love balls!'

Timir fluttered his wings. 'But I was awake and teddies make me snarly and I love bouncing and mud pies and I don't love balls!'

Luma glared at Timir.

Timir glared right back at her, his nostrils wide and snorting.

'Now, now, Timir,' Nani said, bending down to scratch under Timir's chin. 'I know it doesn't seem fair, but Luma is right.'

'No!' Timir whimpered. 'I do not want to be a dog.'

'You don't have to be all the time,' Luma said.

Nani nodded. 'When it is just you and Luma, you can do all the things you love as much as you want.'

'But, Nani?' Luma asked. 'How exactly *do* dogs behave? Because I thought it was completely normal for Timir to bounce on the trampoline and watch the telly. How am I supposed to help Timir be a dog if I don't know what a real dog is like?'

'Don't worry.' Nani smiled. 'I was going to tell you earlier but I didn't get a chance with the boys being here.'

'Tell me what?' Luma asked.

'Well,' Nani said. 'The other day when I was out, I happened to see an advert in a shop window for puppy-training classes.'

'Training classes!' Luma said. 'Ooh! That would be perfect – I could watch the other dogs *and* it might help you to listen to me better, Timir!'

Timir looked up from licking the empty biscuit plate, crumbs falling from his snout.

'My thoughts exactly, Luma,' Nani chuckled. 'Which is why, as soon as I got home, I called the number on the advert and booked you and Timir a place for this afternoon. In fact,' Nani said, glancing at the clock on the wall, 'it starts in one hour, so we had better hurry up!'

* ✭ *

Chapter Eight

Nani left to get ready and Luma fetched her backpack, pulling out the harness and lead.

'You have to let me put it on,' Luma told Timir. 'All the other dogs in the class will be wearing one.'

Timir's wings drooped down behind him, his bottom lip wobbling.

'It won't be that bad,' Luma said. 'Look, this bit goes here.' She looped the harness over his head, but it didn't fit.

'How silly of me,' Luma said. 'You have to be a dog to wear it.'

Timir let out a little rumble but soon transformed.

Luma easily slipped it on.

'And now . . . I'm not too sure, actually. Maybe you could roll on to your back?'

Timir lay down and was very patient indeed while Luma struggled to fix the straps together.

'There, I think it is done now,' Luma said.

Timir remained perfectly still, his four little legs sticking straight in the air.

'I don't like it,' Timir said.

'Maybe you should try standing up?' Luma suggested.

Timir slowly rolled on to his front and stood up. 'I don't like it.'

'What about if you tried walking?'

Timir took two steps forward and then flumped on the floor.

Luma picked up the lead. 'Come on, then,' she said, giving it a gentle tug. 'Let's go.'

They followed Nani outside to her car and after a short drive, they arrived at a park.

It was one Luma had never been to before. She could see a great stretch of green grass and, beyond that, a forest of dark, dense trees.

'It must be over there,' Nani said, pointing towards a square fenced-off area, right before the start of the forest. Inside were five people, four holding leads to various-sized dogs.

'Can we run, Nani?'

'Of course,' Nani chuckled.

'Let's race!' Luma said to Timir.

Luma set off but was soon stopped by a strong tug on the lead.

Timir had dug his claws into the grass, his whole body trembling.

'What's wrong? You love to race,' Luma asked.

'I'm scared,' Timir whispered, for he too had seen the strangers with their dogs in the distance. Timir had never met any dogs before.

'It will be OK,' Luma said, bending

down to stroke his fluffy back. She could feel the slight bumps where his spiky horns usually were. 'I will be with you.'

They walked very slowly down a winding path, all the way to a wooden gate.

'Hello,' said a man, coming towards them. 'My name is George and I am the trainer. You must be Luma and Timir – come on in.'

'I will be over there reading my book,' Nani said, nodding towards a park bench under a nearby tree.

'Bye, Nani,' Luma said.

'Bye, Nani,' Timir whispered.

'Why don't you line up with the others,' the trainer told Luma.

Luma looked at the other dogs and

grinned. This was her first chance to see how an actual dog behaved.

They walked past a tall woman wearing a flowery skirt. She was holding the lead of a large, grey dog. The dog was whining and straining towards the gate.

Next, Luma passed a short man with large, black glasses. There was a rather

plump, wrinkly dog sitting on his foot, looking just as worried as Timir.

Then there was another lady, a fluffy, golden dog panting and drooling at her side.

Finally, there was a girl a few years older than Luma, with long brown hair and the smallest dog Luma had ever seen

shivering behind her leg.

'Hmm,' Luma said to Timir as they stood between the lady and the girl. 'The dogs are all doing different things.'

'Right, everyone!' the trainer said. 'Let's go round and tell each other who we are and then we can begin.'

Timir quaked in Luma's arms and buried himself under her jumper.

* ✳ *

Chapter Nine

Luma didn't get a chance to listen as the other owners introduced themselves – she was too busy trying to get Timir to stop hiding.

'You have to sit on the grass like all the other dogs,' Luma whispered.

Timir did not answer.

And then it was Luma's turn.

'My name is Luma and this is Timir,' she said, pointing towards the Timir-shaped lump under her top.

'How about you pop him down?' the trainer said.

'He doesn't want to,' Luma said.

'I think I have something here that will tempt him,' the trainer said, patting a black pouch around his waist.

The trainer came towards them, taking out a little treat shaped like a dog's paw and waving it in front of Timir.

Luma sighed. That would not work. Maybe if it was a chocolate-chip biscuit?

But to Luma's surprise, Timir's nose poked out.

Timir did a big sniff. 'What is this?'

The trainer moved his hand closer.

Timir stuck out his tongue and gave the treat a lick.

'What a funny tongue he has!' the trainer said. 'What breed of dog is he?'

'Um . . .'

Luma was saved from answering by Timir twisting out of her arms and dropping on to the grass.

He immediately rose up on his back legs, eager to get the treat.

'Everyone look!' the trainer said. 'The first command we will be learning today is "sit".' The trainer held up his hand towards Timir. 'Sit, Timir!'

Timir let out a little whine and . . . sat!

'Good boy, and now you can have this.' The trainer allowed Timir to gobble up the treat and then passed Luma three more. 'Keep practising,' he said, as he walked off.

Luma copied the trainer, once, twice, three times. Timir was sitting perfectly.

'I do it again!' Timir said, rushing to sit down with his mouth open wide.

'I don't have another treat,' Luma said.

Timir stood back up. 'Then I will not sit.'

'Timir.' Luma tutted. 'You can't always have a treat every time you do something.'

'Why?' Timir asked.

'You would get very full up, for a start,' Luma said.

'I would not.' Timir snorted.

'Well, you need to do things just because I ask, not because you want a treat,' Luma said. 'But now we know how to do sit, let's watch the other dogs again.'

Luma turned to look at the woman with the large grey dog at the start of the line.

The dog was glancing about, every so often doing a big bouncing jump.

'Why don't you look around and bounce?' Luma said.

Timir did a quick look and a hop and then his eyes became fixed on the trainer's hand as it moved back and forth from the treat pouch.

'Yum,' Timir said.

'We have to concentrate, Timir,' Luma said. 'Let's watch that one.'

Luma pointed towards the plump, wrinkly dog. It was rolling about in the grass, its tail wagging back and forth.

'Why don't you try a roll and wiggle your tail?' Luma suggested.

Timir did a hurried roll and flop of his tail.

'And what about that one,' Luma said, watching the golden dog as it sat completely still by its owner's side. 'That dog is being very good—'

The golden dog began to bark, great big booming woofs echoing in Luma's ears.

'No, don't copy that dog,' she said. 'Maybe try another look about and a hop and some more rolls and tail wags?'

Timir looked and hopped and rolled and shook his tail.

'Good job, everyone.' The trainer moved to stand in front of the group. 'Now we can move on to "lie down"!'

Timir lay down at once. 'Treat?'

★ ✹ ★

Chapter Ten

The trainer stared at Timir, a puzzled frown on his face. 'Have you been practising that one at home?' he asked.

'I think he just lay down,' Luma said, nudging Timir and trying to get his attention.

'Hmm,' the trainer said and then he set off to help the others.

'But my treat,' Timir whined.

'You can't do that!' Luma said. 'None of the other dogs lay down without being taught how to first.'

Timir did not listen.

He kept trying to catch the trainer's eye, standing up and lying down and standing up and lying down again.

'Stop, Timir, please,' Luma said.

The trainer came to help the young girl and her tiny black dog beside them.

'Good,' the trainer said, holding a treat out as the dog shivered and lay down.

Timir could not take it a second more.

He flew in the air and grabbed the treat out of the trainer's hand!

'Timir!' Luma said.

'Oh dear!' the trainer said.

'**Arwwf!**' the tiny dog groaned.

Timir roared. 'More, I need more!'

'I think you have had enough,' the trainer said to Timir.

Timir howled and then he did something very, *very* naughty.

Timir hunched down and sprang, clamping his teeth around the strap of the treat bag and ripping it off the trainer's waist!

'Timir! Drop that at once!'
Luma cried.

Timir gave Luma a guilty look and
then he twirled away from the trainer's

hands trying to catch him, one treat dropping to the ground.

Timir looked at the treat but his mouth was full of the treat bag.

The tiny dog scooted in, gulping it down.

Timir snarled and took off, racing past the line of dogs, the treats flying left and right.

The fluffy golden dog lurched after Timir, his lead slipping from the lady's hand as he eagerly gobbled up the fallen treats.

Then the plump, wrinkly dog charged forward, its owner nearly falling over as the lead shot from his hand.

The large, grey dog began woofing and bouncing and pulling so hard, its owner squealed and let go of its lead.

And soon all three dogs were sprinting after Timir and the trail of treats!

✦ ✶ ✦

Chapter Eleven

'Everyone, call your dogs!'

The trainer ran after the racing dogs, the owners' cries of 'Bertie' and 'Maisie' and 'Rupert' following him.

One by one, they stopped and allowed their owners to catch them.

Timir, however, did not stop.

He carried on, round and round, until eventually he noticed he was no longer being chased.

He stopped then, dropping the treat bag and nosing inside only to sit up and wail. 'Gone! They've all gone!'

Luma ran to Timir.

'Treats all gone,' Timir said.

Luma crossed her arms. 'That was very naughty.'

The trainer retrieved his empty pouch and tied it back around his waist.

'I think after that we should move on to recall,' the trainer said. 'That means making sure your dog listens when you call for him, every single time, no matter what is distracting them!'

There were a couple of titters and laughs, but also some glares at Timir.

Luma looked towards Nani. This wasn't going very well at all. Timir was still only listening when he chose to. But it seemed Nani had not noticed the chase. Luma could see her smiling as she read her book on the bench under the tree.

'As we don't have any treats left,' the trainer said, walking over to a bag by the gate, 'we will have to use tennis balls to encourage our dogs instead.'

Timir groaned. 'I don't like balls!'

Luma quickly turned away from Nani and back to Timir. 'Remember, all dogs like balls.'

But then the girl next to her spoke. 'Maudie doesn't like tennis balls. They are too big for her little mouth.'

'Ah, in that case…' The trainer ruffled around in the bag, his hand coming out seconds later with a small rubber duck, just like the ones Luma had in her bath.

'I like ducks!' Timir said.

'Timir doesn't like balls either,' Luma said to the trainer.

'I have a second one somewhere in here,' the trainer said.

Luma grinned. Not all dogs liked balls after all. She couldn't wait to tell Arjun. But her smile quickly faded as Timir started crying out for his duck.

'What a strange noise!' the girl said. 'He sounds like a horse whinnying.'

'Or a sheep bleating,' said the woman with the golden dog.

Luma looked about – all the owners and even their dogs were staring at Timir.

'Shush, Timir! Everyone's looking,' Luma whispered.

The trainer came towards them, handing one duck to the girl and one to Luma.

Timir barely waited a second before grabbing it out of Luma's hand.

'**Ow!**' Luma cried.

But Timir was too busy gnawing on the duck to notice.

'Now for recall,' the trainer said.

Each owner took it in turns to hand their dog to the trainer and walk far away, before calling their dog's name.

Luma tried to watch how the dogs

behaved when they were left, but she was starting to think it was pointless. It wasn't what the dogs did that Timir needed to copy, but what the dogs *didn't* do. And no matter what she did or said, Timir would not listen to her when it really mattered.

'Luma, your turn,' the trainer said

Luma passed the trainer Timir's lead, the duck firmly in Timir's mouth.

'Leave it!' the trainer said.

Timir snarled.

'Maybe he can keep the duck for now,' the trainer said.

Luma walked away as the other owners had done. 'Timir, come!' she called.

The trainer unclipped Timir's lead.

Timir wandered off, almost going in Luma's direction, but then he lay down on the grass and began to chew the rubber duck.

'Call him again,' the trainer said.

'Timir!' Luma shouted.

Timir glanced at Luma and then he sat up, the duck falling from his mouth. His ears began to twist back and forth as he stared at something in the distance.

Luma turned to see what Timir was looking at . . .

'Oh no!'

For there was a squirrel, right at the back of the fence, its bushy tail held high. And in its front paws it was holding one of the fallen treats!

Chapter Twelve

'Squirrel.' Timir's eyes narrowed.

Timir became a fluffy blur as he raced towards the squirrel.

The squirrel took one look at Timir and dashed off, jumping over the fence and shooting off into the dense forest of trees.

'Don't worry,' the trainer called to Luma. 'Timir won't be able to get past the fence. Now, this is a very good opportunity to practise recall.'

Timir did stop at the fence.

He paced up and down and . . . wriggled through a gap at the bottom!

'**No! Timir!**' Luma cried, racing

towards the fence. **'Come back!
Come back!'**

Luma reached the fence and climbed over, racing off to where she'd seen Timir disappear.

'Luma, stay here!' she heard the trainer shout. 'We will find him together!'

But Luma could not stop.

She saw a flash of his dragon tail amongst the trees and ran.

And then there was a growl in the other direction.

Luma turned around and sprinted

towards the noise, but Timir wasn't there.

Luma sped further and further into the dense forest of trees.

'Timir!' she shouted. **'Timir!'**

There was silence.

Too much silence.

No growls or squeaks from Timir to tell her where to go next.

But worse, there was no chatter from the other owners, no woofs from their dogs or even calls of her name.

Luma walked around in a slow circle. She wasn't sure which direction she had come from and had no idea which direction she should go.

She was lost.

Luma sat on the ground and burst into tears.

'Oh, Timir,' she cried. 'Where have you gone and how will we find our way back?'

Luma wiped her tears away and that was when she noticed something. A light, coming from somewhere, just like when Timir had run after the squirrel in the morning.

Luma stood up, carefully looking around her.

Where was the light coming from?

She tried walking forwards.

The light dimmed.

She stepped back and it glowed.

'How strange,' Luma said, but she had a feeling inside. The light was important, she just knew it.

Luma looked all around her and then . . .

'Of course!' she cried, seeing the twinkling at her side. 'The charm bracelet!'

★ ✦ ★

Chapter Thirteen

Luma slipped the bracelet off her wrist to examine it more closely.

It was the little black and gold dragon charm that was glowing.

Luma thought back to that morning. She had seen the light when Timir was far from her and it had started flashing just before Timir came out of the tall, tall trees.

Luma had an idea.

She walked straight ahead and, just as she expected, the glow dimmed.

She turned around and walked in the opposite direction and the glow became brighter.

'I knew it!' Luma said. 'The charm is telling me where to go!'

Luma kept walking, keeping the bracelet in front of her. Every time the glow dimmed, she changed direction until it shone again.

Soon enough, it was shining so bright she could have used it as a torch!

And then, finally, the charm began to flash.

Luma held her breath. She heard a rustle behind a tree and then there was Timir, running towards her.

'Timir!'

'Luma!' Timir howled, jumping into her arms.

Luma fell backwards, Timir landing on her chest and licking her face all over.

'Oh, Timir, I thought I had lost you.'

'I was lost,' Timir said. 'The squirrel ran with my treat and I chased, but then the squirrel was gone and . . . and . . .' Timir wailed.

'Shush, now,' Luma said, cuddling Timir closer. 'I'm here and the bracelet helped me find you.'

'We go back now?' Timir asked, staring up at her.

Luma shook her head. 'I don't know where we are at all, Timir.'

Timir sat up and moved off Luma's lap. He put his nose to the ground and began to sniff.

'What is it, Timir?'

Timir stared straight ahead. 'Nani,' he said. 'This way.'

✦ ✭ ✦

Chapter Fourteen

Luma stood up, following Timir as he began to wind his way through the trees.

Timir carried on with his sniffs, stopping every so often to take an enormous gulp of the air.

'Close, now,' Timir said.

And then Luma heard their names being called.

'Luma!' 'Timir!'

'Nani!' Luma shouted, recognising Nani's voice amongst the others.

Luma and Timir ran together. They turned one more corner and there was Nani, looking terribly worried.

'Oh, my little ones!' she cried as they raced towards them. 'Thank goodness.'

'I'm sorry, Nani,' Luma said. 'Timir raced off and I followed him and then I got lost but the bracelet showed me where to find Timir and then Timir led us back with his nose!'

'I am very glad you realised what the dragon charm does,' Nani said. 'And for your clever nose, Timir.'

'Clever nose,' Timir cheeped, spinning in a circle.

And then he tipped his head to one side and, with a shake, changed into a dog.

'You found them.' The trainer sighed in relief as he emerged from the trees.

They headed back to the training area, the other owners and dogs joining them on the way. They had all been searching for Luma and Timir.

'I think I had better find Timir's lead,' the trainer said, once they were inside.

'I will not run away again,' Timir said.

'He won't run away again, not ever,' Luma said for him.

'I should hope not,' the trainer said. 'Why don't we try one more recall to make sure.'

Luma began to walk. Timir immediately followed her.

'Stay, Timir,' Luma told him.

Timir whined but stayed by the trainer's side.

'Come!' Luma called when she was far enough away.

Timir started to run, but then he stopped. The duck was still in the middle where he had left it. Timir gave it a quick sniff and then carried on, racing as fast as he could to Luma.

'Well done, Timir!' Luma cried, picking him up and cuddling him.

Chapter Fifteen

They waved goodbye to everyone and soon they were back in the car, driving home.

'What an adventure!' Nani said. 'A bit more than I thought when I booked the class!'

'Yes,' Luma agreed, stroking Timir's tummy as he snuggled next to her. 'But I did realise something. All dogs behave differently and as long as Timir doesn't do anything too obvious and listens when I tell him to stop—'

'I listen, Luma!' Timir said.

'Good,' Luma said. 'Because then I can tell Arjun that you are completely normal and maybe it's just because he hasn't met many dogs . . . oh, and not all dogs like tennis balls, either!'

Nani laughed. 'Well, I am very pleased and I was *very* impressed you worked out what the dragon charm did by yourself.'

Luma grinned, holding her wrist up to see the bracelet twinkling in the light. 'You did say the charms would help when I needed them most.'

They arrived home. Luma and Timir spent the rest of the afternoon and evening colouring in, doing their jigsaw puzzle (Timir tried to chew up a piece but let it go as soon as Luma asked), playing songs on their recorder and drum, and finally watching more cartoons. Then Mum arrived to collect them.

'So, what have you two been up to

today?' Mum asked as they walked home. 'Other than getting Timir on a lead,' she said, smiling at Timir beside them.

'We went to a puppy-training class,' Luma said.

'You did? How fantastic!'

'Yes, although we got lost, but it's OK,' Luma said quickly, as she saw Mum's face fall. 'We found each other and then Nani.'

'Oh,' Mum said. 'And what did you and Timir learn?'

Luma waited until they were inside their house to show Mum.

'Watch, Mum . . . Timir, sit!'

Timir sat.

'Lie down.'

Timir lay down.

'And stay!' Luma walked all the way to the other end of the hall. 'Come!'

Timir ran towards Luma, jumping into her arms.

'Very well done,' Mum said. 'And now I think it is time for a bath and then bed.'

'Rubber duck?' Timir asked Luma.

'Yes, you can chew up an entire one to yourself!'

After her bath and their bedtime story, Luma cuddled Timir as they lay tucked up in bed.

She could already feel her eyes beginning to close. It had been a very long and busy day, but there was just one more thing she had to do before she fell asleep.

'Timir?'

'Yes?' Timir yawned.

'In the morning, do you promise to go back to sleep if I say, or at least play very quietly so I can sleep?'

She felt Timir let out a little rumble.

'Promise,' he said finally, snuggling closer to her. 'I love you, Luma.'

'I love you, Timir.' Luma smiled. 'Night night.

Luma and Timir's Top Tips for Pet Care

There are many human foods that are not good for animals. It is always important to check a new food is safe before giving it to your pet.

'Dogs definitely can't eat chocolate,' Luma says. 'It's poisonous to them.'

'No!' Timir howls.

'It's ok, you can, because you are mostly dragon.'

Animals like dogs need lots and lots of exercise and play to keep them happy.
Luma says, 'You could take your dog to the park, around the roads, or play in your garden with a ball . . .'

'I do not like balls,' Timir says.

'But you chase your duck teddy. That is the same thing.'

'I love duck teddy, I am not chasing him, I am rescuing him from you throwing him!'

Make sure your animal has regular feeding times and always, always has plenty of fresh water.

'Water is especially important when it is hot outside,' Luma says.

'And ice cream,' Timir says. 'Ice cream is very important when it is hot.'

'But pets shouldn't have ice cream. Remember about human foods?'

'Oh... ice cream is very important when you have a *dragon* and it's hot.'

Animals need their own beds or special place, somewhere nice and cool for the summer and lovely and warm for the winter.

'But my bed is your bed,' Timir says. 'It is our bed.'

Luma says, 'You do have your own bed too.'

'That is duck teddy's bed and zebra teddy's and panda teddy's *and* my yo-yo's bed.'

All animals need buckets of love.
'Tummy tickles are the best,' Timir says.

'And ear scratching,' Luma says. 'You love that.'

'And kisses.'

'And snuggling.'

'And lots and lots and lots of cuddling!'

Leah Mohammed lives in Sunbury-on-Thames, Surrey, with her daughter and their much-loved dogs, Henry, the Chorkie, and Maudie, the teeny and often shivering Chihuahua. After studying for a degree in psychology and a masters in psychotherapy, Leah worked as a therapist before deciding to concentrate on her love of writing. Coming from a mixed cultural background, Leah's hope is to introduce diverse characters and explore different types of family dynamics in stories for everyone to enjoy.

Loretta Schauer originally trained as
a dancer, then managed a conservation charity
on Hampstead Heath for many years – battling
brambles by day, and practising her drawing skills
by night. She won the Waterstone's 'Picture This'
competition in 2011 and has since illustrated
picture books and fiction titles for a wide range
of publishers. Loretta lives in North London at
the top of a very tall building with her husband
and pet hamster. She occasionally escapes to
go galloping around in the mud, swimming in
the ponds, or noodling for fossils. One day she
hopes to live beside the seaside with a garden
full of chickens and guinea pigs.

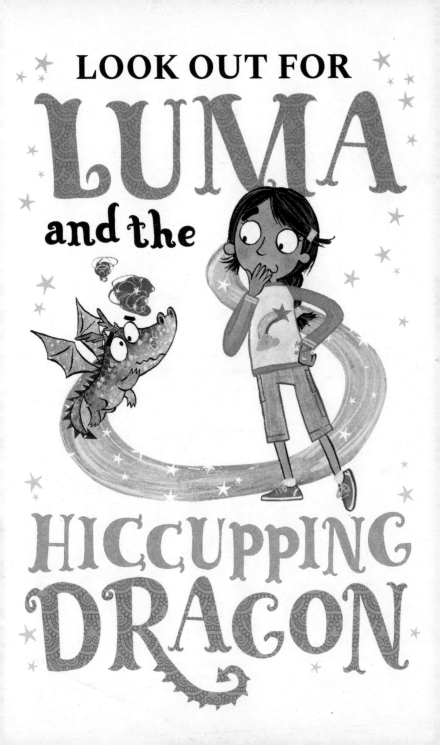

LOOK OUT FOR

LUMA

and the

HICCUPPING DRAGON